Classic

STORYBOOK FABLES

Classic
STORYBOOK FABLES

Illustrated by Scott Gustafson

Artisan | New York

To those grand old men Arthur, Norman, and N.C.
and countless others whose work continues to inspire

Library of Congress Cataloging-in-Publication Data
Names: Gustafson, Scott, illustrator.
Title: Classic storybook fables / illustrated by Scott Gustafson.
Description: New York : Artisan, 2017. | Summary: An illustrated retelling of
   eight classic fairy tales, emphasizing the lesson to be learned from each.
Identifiers: LCCN 2016058707 | ISBN 9781579657048 (hardback, with dust jacket)
Subjects: LCSH: Fairy tales. | CYAC: Fairy tales. | Folklore.
Classification: LCC PZ8.G97 Sto 2017 | DDC 398.2 [E] —dc23 LC record available at
https://lccn.loc.gov/2016058707

Design adapted from Bjorn Akselsen

For more information about Scott Gustafson's illustration and books, please visit scottgustafson.com.

Artisan books are available at special discounts when purchased in bulk for premiums and sales promotions as well as for fund-raising or educational use. Special editions or book excerpts also can be created to specification. For details, contact the Special Sales Director at the address below, or send an e-mail to specialmarkets@workman.com.

Published by Artisan
A division of Workman Publishing Co., Inc.
225 Varick Street
New York, NY 10014-4381
artisanbooks.com

Artisan is a registered trademark of Workman Publishing Co., Inc.

Published simultaneously in Canada by Thomas Allen & Son, Limited

Printed in China

10 9 8 7 6 5 4 3 2

Contents

The Ugly Duckling

IT WAS A GLORIOUS SUMMER DAY. The birds sang, and the sun glistened off the water in the canal. In the reeds at the water's edge, a mother duck sat on her nest full of eggs. She had been sitting there, keeping her eggs safe and warm, day after day, for what seemed like forever, as she waited for them to hatch.

But this day, with the sun shining so brightly and a wonderful breeze rippling the water, she didn't feel like waiting there all alone anymore. What she wanted to do was jump into the water and join the other ducks, who were swimming and quacking in the canal. But she knew she had to stay put until her eggs were ready to hatch.

Suddenly, one of the eggs began to move and crack, and that egg was soon joined by another and then another. As little beaks poked their way through broken eggshells, the "peep, peep" of tiny ducklings filled the air. Before long, the new arrivals were exploring their surroundings. Compared with the insides of their eggs, the family nest seemed huge!

"So you think this little piece of the world is big, do you?" the mother duck said with a smile. "Wait until you see the barnyard and the pasture that runs all the way down to the parson's farm!" Then she noticed that the biggest egg had not hatched.

"Hello there," quacked a familiar voice. It was one of the other barnyard ducks, paddling by for a visit. "You've got some new arrivals, I see."

"Yes, all except one," answered the mother duck. "This big one seems to be taking its time."

"Ah," said the visitor as she craned her neck to get a better look at the uncooperative egg. "I bet that's a turkey egg. One of those got mixed up in my clutch once, and I was fooled into hatching it. Good luck!" she said as she swam away.

The mother duck sighed and settled back onto the egg. It wasn't long before her wait was over. The last egg started to move, and soon it cracked open and a large, funny-looking duckling tumbled out. The mother duck immediately noticed that this duckling was different from the others. He was sort of a gray color, and though she hated to admit it, even to herself, he wasn't as cute as the rest of her brood. In fact, this poor little thing was rather ugly.

The other ducklings were quick to notice the new arrival's differences, too. "Hey!" they peeped meanly. "Look at the big one. He's goofy-looking!"

The mother duck stepped in and told the others they had to be nice to their newest brother, but she couldn't help thinking that there was some truth in what they had said.

The next day, the mother duck led her brood down to the water's edge for a swimming lesson. As each duckling plopped in, its head went underwater, but soon each little bird bobbed to the surface and began to paddle around. When the ugly duckling's turn came, the mother duck held her breath. *Plop*, in he went, and just like the others, he bobbed to the surface and started to paddle. But soon it was clear that here, too, he was different. He could swim faster and farther than the others.

"Look what a fine swimmer we have here," thought the mother duck, "and how elegantly he holds himself in the water! He is actually quite handsome, when you really stop to look at him." The next day, proud and eager to show off her little brood, she took the ducklings to the farm. But as soon as they reached the barnyard, the other birds began to say rude things and peck at the ugly duckling.

"Hey, leave him alone," said his mother. "He wasn't bothering you!"

"Well," clucked a haughty hen, "we don't like him. He's strange-looking!"

"That's no reason to be cruel," said the mother duck.

"You may be right," quacked a wise old duck. "But you have to admit, dear, he doesn't really look like the rest of your family."

"He was the last one hatched and may have spent a little too much time in the egg," said the mother duck. "But he's very good-natured and a wonderful swimmer." And yet no matter what she said, as soon as her back was turned, the others continued to call him names and peck at the gawky duckling. Even his brothers and sisters joined in, making the poor thing feel unwelcome and unwanted. Every day it grew worse and worse, until he could take no more.

One morning, the ugly duckling slipped through a hole in the fence and struck out into the wide world. As he waddled and stumbled through the undergrowth, wild birds chirped and quickly flew away.

"They must be flying off because I'm so ugly," the sad duckling thought. Late in the day, he found himself in a marsh, where he took shelter for the night in the rushes at the water's edge.

The next morning, a pair of wild ducks and their ducklings came paddling by.

"Well, what have we here?" quacked the mother.

"I must say, I've never seen anything quite like this in our neighborhood before," said her husband.

"I guess he can stay," said the mother. "As long as he doesn't get any ideas about joining *our* family."

"We definitely can't have that!" the father agreed, and the ducks gave their beaks a superior tilt as they proudly swam by.

The poor duckling didn't want to join anybody else's family; he just wanted a place to stay. Moments later, two wild geese splashed down onto the water nearby. They were young and boisterous, honking and laughing as they swam.

"Hey!" said one of them as they headed toward the duckling. "Look at this!"

"Yeah," said the other. "The guy's kind of funny-looking, but you know what? That's what I like about him!"

"Hey, buddy," said the first goose to the duckling. "There's a flock of us in the next marsh over, a really great bunch of guys. Anyway, we're all getting ready to fly south for the winter. Want to come along?"

But before the duckling could answer, there was a loud boom.

"Yikes!" honked the second goose. "Hunters!" With a great splash and flurry, the two flapped off into the sky.

BOOM! Another shot was fired, and the duckling scurried into the reeds. All of a sudden, a dog thrust his head through the weeds. His big nose and drooling mouth were just inches from where the duckling cowered. The dog looked at him for a frightening moment, then snorted and ran off in the opposite direction, just as another shot rang out.

"Phew!" the duckling sighed in relief. "I guess this time I was lucky to be so ugly—even that dog didn't want to have anything to do with me."

After the smoke had cleared and the hunters had gone, the duckling remained hidden. He waited quite some time before he felt it was safe to come out.

"There's got to be a better place to live than this," he thought. So once more, he struck out into the wide world. By evening, he found himself in the yard of a run-down farm cottage. The old building leaned this way and that, as if it couldn't decide which way to fall—yet somehow, it remained standing. The smell of something cooking drew the duckling closer, and he wriggled through a gap beneath the cottage's front door.

Inside, an old woman dozed by a cozy fire with her companions: an old hen and a cat. The hen had a talent for laying eggs, which made her dear to the old woman's heart. The cat not only caught mice but also purred when he was happy and hissed when he was angry, all of which pleased the old woman to no end. Together, they lived quite happily in the tumbledown cottage. The duckling found an out-of-the-way corner, and he, too, settled in for the night.

The next morning when the old woman discovered the visitor, her poor old eyes mistook him for a much older duck. "This is lucky," she said, "for if this duck can lay eggs, we could have fresh duck eggs to eat." So she planned to let the duckling stay for a while to see if it would produce any eggs.

"Can you lay eggs?" the hen asked the duckling.

"No," he replied.

"How about catching mice or purring?" asked the cat.

"I can't do those things either," the duckling answered.

"Well, then just sit in the corner and keep your mouth shut when your betters are speaking," said the hen. So the duckling sat quietly in the corner, feeling as if he had done something wrong.

Several days later, the sun shone so cheerfully through the window that it reminded the duckling of summer days on the pond, and he asked the hen if she had ever gone swimming.

"What a question!" the hen replied. "You not only look peculiar but you say peculiar things. Well, I've got a question for you. Can you lay eggs yet?"

"No," said the duckling.

"Then you'd better go," said the hen.

"Before you're cooked for dinner," added the cat.

So once more, the duckling struck out into the wide world. The cold wind
was blowing more sharply now, and the leaves were turning to yellow, orange, and
red. Autumn had come, and the poor duckling wandered aimlessly, looking for food
and shelter.

Soon winter arrived. The weather turned colder, and then colder still, and the duckling took refuge in a small pond. As the edges of the pond froze, the duckling kept swimming around in circles to keep the water free from ice until, exhausted, he could swim no more. The next morning, he awoke to find his legs frozen fast in the solid ice.

Luckily, a poor peasant found him and, after breaking the duckling free from the ice, carried him home to his cottage. There, the peasant and his wife put the duckling in a crate that they placed near the fire. The couple's children, excited to have a new pet in the house, fed the duckling every day. They constantly begged to be allowed to take the bird out of his crate so they could play with him, but the answer was always no.

As the days went by and the duckling regained his strength, he, too, wondered when he would be set free from the confines of the crate. One evening, just before dinner, when their father was out gathering firewood and their mother was in the barn, the children opened the crate and coaxed the duckling out. As the bird emerged from his pen, the children began to laugh and clap their hands.

This startled the poor duckling and, in a panic, he ran about the small kitchen, flapping his wings.

Just then, the children's mother returned from the barn. "Oh, no!" she cried. Soon the entire family was chasing the poor, confused duckling from one side of the room to the other. Terrified, he ran across the table, sending plates and utensils flying. He ran through the butter pot, overturned the milk pitcher, then landed in the bean bin.

"Open the door, Fritz!" the frantic mother called to her son. Then, waving a large wooden spoon, she chased the frightened duckling out into the cold dark night and slammed the door shut behind him.

The rest of that winter, the duckling searched for food by day and huddled under rushes by night. After many weeks, the snow and ice melted— spring had come at last.

One warm spring day, the duckling realized that his wings had grown, and when he flapped them, he rose into the air.

Soon he was flying short distances, and before long, and without even quite
knowing how he'd gotten there, he found himself in a beautiful park. There he saw
fragrant apple trees blossoming and willows bending over the banks of a lovely river
that wound its way through the park. As he swam across the water, two majestic
swans came into view from around a bend. Even at this distance, he was in awe of
their beauty and embarrassed by his own ugliness. Wishing he could disappear, he
lowered his head in shame.

There, in the glassy shimmer of the water, he saw something unbelievable.
Looking back at him from the mirror-like surface was not the gawky creature he
had expected to see but a graceful white bird. He spread his wings, and the
magnificent reflection did the same. It was true: the ugly duckling had grown into
a beautiful swan!

The other swans approached and welcomed him. Children playing in the park spotted him and cried, "There's a new swan, and he is even more beautiful than the others!" They threw bread and morsels of food to the swans and laughed excitedly as the regal birds glided near them.

Through it all, the duckling moved as if in a dream. After all the hard times and disappointments he had known, it was difficult to believe that he had really come to such a wonderful place. The once lonely and frightened little creature could never have imagined that he would one day be so completely transformed. When he raised his graceful neck and ruffled his snow-white feathers in the warm sunlight, he did so not out of pride but with a spirit of thankfulness and joy. Because now he realized that it didn't matter if you were born an ugly duckling, as long as a beautiful swan awaited within.

Beauty and the Beast

ONCE UPON A TIME there was a very rich merchant who had three daughters. The girls were all pretty, but the youngest was so striking that even as a child, she was given the nickname "Beauty." As she grew, the name continued to suit her, so Beauty she remained. She was not only beautiful to look at but a lovely person on the inside as well, and everyone who knew her adored her. Everyone, that is, except her two sisters, who were envious of her in every way. Where she was humble and kind, they were proud and cruel.

One day, without warning, the merchant lost his fortune. Overnight, the once wealthy family was forced to move from their luxurious mansion in the city to the merchant's only remaining property: a humble farm in the country. The man went from being a gentleman in fine clothes to being a laborer in the fields.

Beauty's life also changed. The girls' mother had died when Beauty was a young girl, and now, from early morning until well after dark, she alone cooked, sewed, cleaned, and did the thousand-and-one things it took to keep a household running smoothly. Even though her new life was hard and often made her sad, she learned to take pride in her work, and at the end of a long day, she looked forward to resting by the fire, where she would read to her father or play her harp.

Her sisters, however, could not adapt to this new lifestyle. When they weren't wailing and moaning, they were cross and spiteful. Bored with country life, they

slept late every morning, then expected Beauty to wait on them hand and foot. The young men who had come to call when the sisters were rich no longer cared to visit proud young women who now were poor.

Some time after the family's move to the country, good news arrived: a trading ship that the merchant had invested in, and that was thought to have been lost at sea, had at last returned to port. Anticipating that he would make a profit

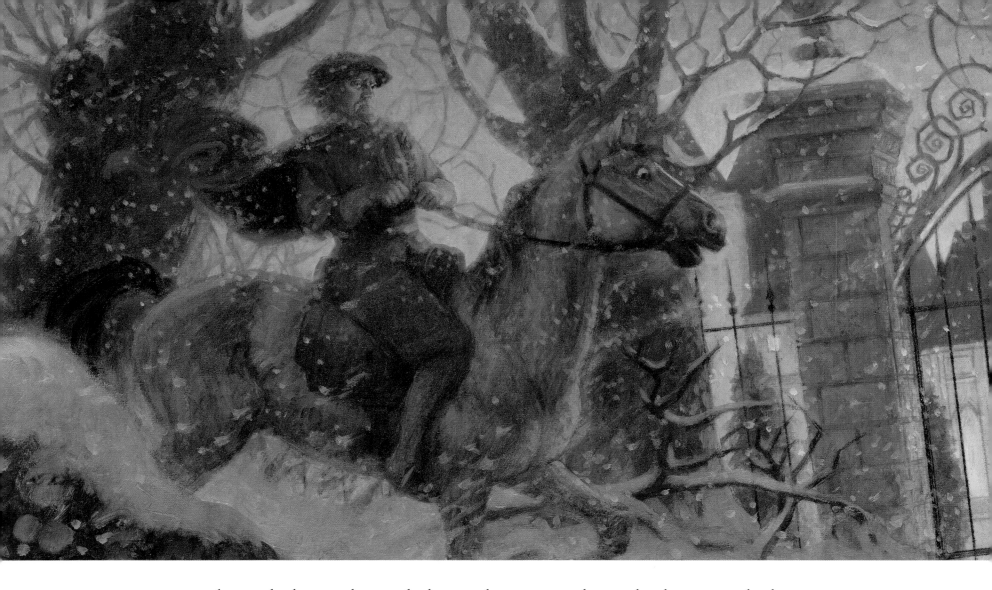

on the goods the vessel carried, the merchant prepared to make the journey back to town. When his older daughters learned that their fortunes would soon be restored, they begged their father to bring back gifts of splendid gowns, expensive shoes, and fine jewelry. Beauty, however, asked for nothing except his safe return.

"Are you sure you don't want anything, Beauty?" her father asked.

Aware that her sisters were growing angry with her for not being as selfish as they were, she answered, "Actually, a rose would be nice. We can't seem to grow them here, and I miss the ones we had in our old garden."

With hugs and kisses and high hopes, the merchant departed. But upon arriving at his destination, he soon learned the sad truth. The vessel had been caught in a storm, and in order to save the ship and crew, much of the cargo had been thrown overboard. Now, between the cost of repairs to the ship and the

sailors' wages, the merchant was even poorer than before. Downhearted, he packed up and headed for home.

On the journey that night, things for the merchant got even worse. He was caught in a blinding snowstorm in a forest thirty miles from home. As the wind howled, he could barely make out the shapes of hungry wolves as they followed him through the woods, waiting for his stumbling horse to slip and fall. Then, miraculously, he caught sight of a light through the trees. Soon he could see that it was not just a single light but an entire mansion, with windows aglow from top to bottom. As he passed through the front gate, the merchant realized that even though it was snowing heavily in the forest, not a single flake fell within the grounds of this estate. And what grounds they were! Manicured gardens, filled with flowers and trees, decorated the landscape.

The merchant found a stable, doors wide open, with a warm, dry stall and plenty of fresh hay and water. His starving horse began to eat. The merchant continued on to the palace, where he hoped to get permission to stay the night.

He knocked at the front door and rang the bell, but no one came. To his surprise, the door was unlocked, so he let himself in. He called out, only to hear the echo fade unanswered. To his left was a lovely room with comfortable chairs pulled up to a welcoming fire. He removed his wet cloak and warmed himself by the fireside. There he waited, expecting sooner or later to be discovered by a servant, but no one came. Exhausted, he dozed off and on in the warm glow. The mantel clock chimed, reminding him of the lateness of the hour, and of how long he had been sitting undisturbed.

Now, quite sure no one was home, he opened the door to an adjoining room, where, to his astonishment, he found a candlelit table covered with every sort of wonderful food, but at which only one place had been set. Overcome with hunger, the merchant sat at the table and ate. Still no one appeared.

"Surely," he thought, "there must be a wonderful fairy who lives here, who is kindly providing everything I need." When he finished eating, he found a turned-down bed and a cheerful fire blazing in a nearby room.

"You are most kind, good fairy," he said aloud. He removed his tattered and weather-stained garments, climbed into the bed, and was soon fast asleep. He was amazed the next morning to see that the old clothes he had left on the chair had been replaced by a new, handsomely tailored suit. "Thank you, good fairy!" he said as he dressed. In the room where he had dined the previous evening, he now found a sumptuous breakfast awaiting him. Later, as he walked to the stable, he passed beneath a beautiful trellis covered with the loveliest roses. Reminded of his daughter Beauty, and her simple request, he plucked a single blossom.

Suddenly, from behind him there came a terrifying roar, and he turned to see a horrible monster about to pounce on him.

"How dare you?!" the Beast snarled. "I have saved your life, fed and clothed you, and made you a guest in my house, and you steal the one thing I love the most—my roses! I'll give you fifteen minutes to make your peace with heaven and then you will pay dearly for your thievery!"

"Please!" the merchant cried, and he fell to his knees trembling. "Please, my lord, have pity! I took the rose only as a gift for one of my daughters, Beauty. I had no idea—"

"Ah, so you have daughters, do you?" the Beast growled. "Well, I will spare your life only if one of your daughters will come to take your place. But she must come of her own free will, and before you can go, you must swear to me that if one of them refuses to come, you yourself will return here in seven days."

"I swear!" the frightened man said. The merchant had no intention of letting one of his daughters take his place, but he agreed, if only to have a chance to say good-bye to his children.

Then, as he turned to go, the Beast stopped suddenly, and in a surprisingly kind voice said, "No guest of this house ever goes away empty-handed. You will find a chest in the room where you slept. Fill it with whatever you want, and I will have it sent to your home."

With that, the Beast left him. In the bedroom, the merchant did indeed find a chest, and next to it were pieces of gold and jewels. "Well," he thought, "if I am going to die, at least my children will be provided for." So he placed some gold and jewels in the chest, closed the lid, and went to the stable to get his horse.

When he arrived home, his daughters rushed out to greet him, and as he hugged them, he burst into tears. He handed Beauty the rose that he still held in his hand and then told them the entire story. When he had finished, the older daughters wept and angrily turned on Beauty. "It's all her fault. She just *had* to have a rose!" they sneered. "And look, she hasn't shed a single tear."

"What good will crying do?" replied Beauty, who indeed did not weep like her sisters. "Besides, Father is not going to die. I asked for the rose, and I intend to pay the price by going to the Beast's palace."

"No, Beauty," the merchant said. "I will not hear of you sacrificing your young life for mine."

"Father, it's of no use for you to try to stop me!" Beauty's voice was firm. "I could not live with myself if I knew you had died because of my foolish request."

The merchant knew that it was pointless to argue and was deeply sorry that it had to come to this. His older daughters, on the other hand, were secretly glad, thinking that soon they would finally be rid of their faultless little sister.

That evening when the merchant went to his bedroom, he found the chest that the Beast had promised to send. He asked Beauty what she thought he should do with the treasure.

"While you were away," Beauty said, "two young gentlemen began calling on my sisters. Perhaps it would be best to set aside the money for their dowries. That way, if anything happens, at least they will be taken care of." The merchant thought this was very sound advice and did as she suggested.

All too quickly the seven days passed, and it was time to return to the Beast's palace. The older sisters made a great show of grief as they said good-bye to Beauty, pretending to cry and faint from sorrow. The merchant's horse knew the way, and by nightfall they found themselves at the gates of the Beast's estate. Just as before, the magnificent palace was aglow. Had it not been for the terrifying nature of their visit, Beauty surely would have enjoyed the spectacle. The father and daughter found the gardens, stable, and palace all empty as before—but this time, the banquet table was set for two instead of just one.

"I suppose this Beast wants to fatten me up before he devours me," Beauty thought, so she tried to enjoy what she assumed would be her last meal.

As they finished eating, the Beast suddenly joined them. He was more frightening than she had ever imagined, and his terrifying presence filled even that large chamber. The merchant gasped and couldn't stop himself from crying, for he knew that the moment he had feared the most was now upon them. Beauty trembled with horror but tried desperately to compose herself for her father's sake.

"So, your daughter came after all," said the Beast as he fixed his ferocious gaze upon her. "Tell me, did you come of your own free will?"

She had looked away, but as she answered, her eyes met his. "Yes," she replied.

"Then you are a good daughter," he said in a quiet voice. The tone of his reply surprised Beauty, and for a moment she thought perhaps there was some kindness deep within the Beast after all. But then he turned to her father.

"And you," he said sternly. "You must leave tomorrow morning and never return! Good night, Beauty," he said, then he left as quickly as he had come.

This encounter with the monster had left her father weak and exhausted. As he leaned heavily on her, she helped him into a bed in the next room, where he quickly went to sleep. Beauty found a bed for herself in an adjoining chamber. That night, she dreamed that a lovely woman came to her and said, "Do not fear, Beauty, for your kindness to your father will not go unrewarded." The next morning, she told her father about the dream.

"Perhaps," he said, a bit comforted, "the kind fairy who lives in this enchanted place will help you."

As he prepared to leave, the merchant kept insisting that it was he who should be staying and not his daughter, but Beauty had made up her mind. After many tears and farewell embraces, Beauty watched as her father rode through the gates and pointed his horse toward home. The sadness of seeing her father for the last time overwhelmed the girl, and she wept. As she dried her tears and walked back to the palace, she realized that hiding from the Beast would be useless, so she gathered up her courage and began to walk from room to room. Soon she came to a door over which were written the words "Beauty's Room." Upon entering, she was amazed to find that of all the beautiful rooms in the palace, this was her favorite. There were shelves loaded with books, a closet full of the loveliest gowns, volumes of sheet music, and a large variety of musical instruments—including a harp.

"If the Beast is intending to kill me," thought Beauty, "it seems strange that he would go to all this trouble to make my life so pleasant." She removed a book from the shelf and found an elegant gold inscription inside:

Beauty,
Everything within this house is at your command.
Ask for anything you wish.

"Ah," Beauty sighed, "as beautiful as all of this is, my only true wish is to see my poor father once again."

As she spoke, the reflection in a nearby mirror grew foggy. Out of the mist appeared her father, stooped with sadness as he rode into their farmyard. Her sisters rushed out to meet him. Even though they pretended to be sad that Beauty was not with him, she could see in their faces that they were secretly glad to be rid of her. The image faded, then disappeared altogether.

Beauty was grateful that the Beast had allowed her to see her father again. "Perhaps," she thought, "this monster is kinder than he appears."

At lunchtime, Beauty found a lavish meal laid out for her in the dining room. Even though she ate alone, she enjoyed a lovely concert played by invisible musicians. That evening at dinner, her host finally made an appearance. As she was about to seat herself at the table, Beauty was startled to see the Beast standing in the shadows at the edge of the room.

"May I watch you eat your dinner, Beauty?" the Beast asked softly. Beauty thought that she had prepared herself for anything that might happen when she saw the monster next, but this strange request surprised her. Despite herself, she trembled as she answered, "You are the master here."

"There you are wrong, Beauty," the Beast said, his eyes never leaving her as he spoke, "for you are mistress in this house, and if my presence annoys you, I will go. But tell me," he continued, "do you think that I am very ugly?"

She paused, fearing that her answer might anger the monster, then finally said, "Yes, I'm afraid I do . . . but I say that only because I think you want the truth. I also think you have been very generous."

"I hope that someday you will find me less ugly," said the Beast, "but I also hope that you will never lie to me. And the last thing I want is for you to be unhappy, so please remember that this household and everything in it is yours to command."

"Thank you," said Beauty. "You are indeed very kind, and when I think of that, you are not so frightening."

"I may have a kind heart," the Beast said sadly, "but I am still a monster."

"There are many people who are cruel but are able to hide their monstrosity beneath their human form," said Beauty. "I prefer the company of someone who may appear on the outside to be a monster but is truly gentle and good within."

This touched the Beast deeply. "I wish I could tell you how much what you have said means to me. As it is, I can only ask you this: Beauty, will you be my wife?"

Beauty was taken aback and couldn't help but show her surprise at this question. She looked away, trying to avoid the monster's intense gaze. "No, Beast," she said at last. "I am sorry, but I can't."

The Beast heaved a deep, sad sigh that drifted through the room and echoed down the hallways. "Good night, Beauty," he said as he turned and followed the echo of his own sigh into the darkness.

Alone in the room, Beauty couldn't help but wonder at the strangeness of her new life and marvel at how truly sorry she felt for the most unhappy Beast. Over the next several months, Beauty grew accustomed to her new home. She filled her days with activities and began to look forward to her evenings with the Beast; for every night at nine o'clock, the Beast would join her in the dining room for dinner. Throughout the day she would see or read something and think, "I must remember to tell the Beast about that." Many evenings she would bring a book, and after the meal was cleared away by invisible hands, she would read to him. Or perhaps she would bring her harp and play a new piece she had learned.

Every night, she hoped that whatever new pastime she offered would divert him from asking the same awful question. But every night, even if she read the most wonderful story or played the loveliest music, she could still feel his gaze upon her and see in his sad eyes how deeply his soul ached. Then, as the story ended, or the last note faded, the dreaded question would come: "Beauty, will you be my wife?"

And every night, she replied with the equally dreaded answer: "No, Beast. I can't. . . . "

Then one night, just as he was about to speak, Beauty spoke first. "Beast, please. I know what you are about to ask, and every night, it breaks my heart to give you the same answer. You are my dearest friend, and I hate to hurt you. I care for you so deeply, Beast, but as a friend." Beauty turned her face away, trying to hide her tears.

"Beauty, I have made you unhappy," the Beast said sadly. "I fear only one thing in this life—that you will go away and never return. Because if you do, I will die. I will never ask you that question again if you promise that you will live here forever."

"I will make that promise," Beauty answered, "but first I must ask a favor." Ever since noticing how frail her father looked when she last saw him, she had been worried about his health. "Please, let me see my father once more."

"You can see him tomorrow," the Beast replied. "But if you do not return, I will die."

"I promise to be gone for only one week, and then when I return, I will stay with you always," Beauty said.

"Take this ring," the Beast said as he gave it to her. "You need only turn it around your finger three times before you go to sleep tonight. Tomorrow morning you will awaken in your father's house. In the same way, you can return here anytime you choose. But remember, if you stay away longer than seven days, you will return to find me no more.

"Good-bye, Beauty," said the Beast, but as he started to go, he paused to look at her one last time. It was only a moment, just long enough for Beauty to catch a glimpse of a tear glistening in the monster's eye, and then he was gone.

That night, Beauty followed the Beast's instructions, and the next morning, she awoke in her father's house. The old man laughed and cried with joy as he

hugged his beloved Beauty. Word was sent to her sisters, and soon they arrived with their new husbands. As it turned out, using the dowries that their father had provided, the sisters had managed to find mates who were equal to them in every unpleasant way—equally proud in character and cruel in nature. At first, the sisters pretended to be thrilled to have Beauty back again, but when they saw how elegantly she was dressed and learned how happy she was in her palatial home, they were overcome with envy and soon went back to their old spiteful ways, treating Beauty more like their servant than their sister.

Within days, Beauty had grown weary of their mistreatment and longed to return to the kindness of the Beast. When she told her family that she must leave at the end of the week or her friend would die, the cruel sisters immediately realized how they could destroy her happiness. Suddenly, they were oozing with sweetness. "Oh, little sister," they begged through false tears, "please stay just a few more days—we love you so!"

Beauty was touched. Her whole life, she had so yearned to be cared for by these evil creatures that she fell into their trap. Seven, and then eight, and then nine days passed.

On the night of the ninth day, she had a frightful dream in which she ran through the palace searching in vain for the Beast. Finally, she found him lying on the ground in the garden—dead. She woke up crying, twisted the ring around her finger three times, and drifted back to sleep. When she awoke the next morning, she was home in the palace of the Beast. Just as in her dream, she ran from room to room, hoping to find him. Frantic, she ran into the garden, where her nightmare came true—for there, on the ground by the fountain, lay her Beast.

"Beast!" she cried and ran to him, but he didn't move. She shook him, trying to revive him, but he still didn't respond. In utter despair, she fell onto him and wept. "Oh, Beast!" she cried. "Please don't die! Not now that I finally know how much you mean to me. Not now that I know that I love you! Please, open your eyes and ask me that question again so I can tell you how much I want to be your wife!"

Suddenly, a violent shudder ran through the Beast, and he breathed a long, deep sigh. Fearing this was the end, Beauty jumped back.

The air was filled with a rushing sound, and as she turned to look, the entire palace glowed with a brilliant light, and fireworks lit up the sky. When she turned back, she found a handsome prince lying in the monster's place. His eyes opened, and he sat up.

"Beauty," he said, "your love has saved my life! Many years ago, an evil witch turned me into a beast and said the only way the curse could be broken was if a beautiful woman told me she loved me and would consent to be my wife."

Overjoyed, Beauty gave the Prince her hand and helped him to his feet. Together they entered the light-filled palace. To Beauty's surprise, her family was gathered there. The lovely woman who had appeared to Beauty in her dream was indeed a fairy, and it was she who had worked to help undo the witch's evil spell.

"Beauty," the fairy said, taking her hand, "you will be rewarded not only for your steadfast love and devotion to your father but also for learning to overcome your fear of a beast to find the true, kind heart that beat within. You shall remain in this palace and take your rightful place beside your prince."

"As for you, ladies," the fairy said, turning to the sisters, "your pride and cruelty have earned you quite another reward. You will stand at the palace doors as stone statues and will silently watch your sister's happiness until you realize the pain you have caused and admit your mistakes. You will, I fear, remain statues for a long time."

With a wave of her wand, all was accomplished. The Prince's lands and his subjects were all restored to him. The royal couple ruled with wisdom and kindness and lived happily ever after.

The Crow and the Pitcher

A VERY THIRSTY CROW came upon a pitcher. Having looked far and wide for something to drink, the parched bird peered into the jug.

"At last," she said, "a bit of water." But unfortunately for her, the vessel's narrow neck kept her from reaching the cool water at the bottom, no matter how hard she tried. Discouraged but far from giving up on the possibility of quenching her thirst, she took a moment to think things over.

"Aha!" she cried. "I have an idea!" The crow began picking up nearby pebbles and dropping them into the pitcher. With every stone that plunked into the old jug, the water level was raised just a bit. Pebble by pebble, the clever bird kept raising the level of the water until at last a cool drink was within reach.

"Ah," sighed the refreshed crow, "so it's true. Necessity *is* the mother of invention!"

The Emperor's New Clothes

MANY YEARS AGO, there lived an Emperor who loved new clothes so much that he spent all of his money on fancy outfits. He didn't care much about meeting with his generals or visiting the theater or even going for a ride in the park. He was interested only in showing off the latest addition to his wardrobe.

Life was very merry in the capital city, with new visitors arriving every day. One day, two scoundrels appeared in the city. They told everyone that they were weavers and that they could weave the most beautiful and luxurious cloth imaginable. Not only were the colors rich and the patterns fabulous, they claimed, but the fabric also had the wonderful quality of remaining invisible to anyone who was unfit for his or her position or who was remarkably stupid.

"Now, this must be splendid cloth indeed," the Emperor thought. "Why, if I were to wear a suit made of that cloth, I would know who in my kingdom was unqualified for his job. And I could easily distinguish between the wise and the foolish. I simply must have some of that marvelous fabric woven for me!"

The Emperor ordered that the two weavers be paid a large amount of gold right away, so that they would start work on his clothes without delay. Soon these so-called weavers set up a loom and pretended to be hard at work, but in reality they did nothing, for the loom was empty. They requested spools of the finest threads made from silk and gold, but these were put into their own knapsacks. Then they returned to the empty loom, where they resumed their pretend work until late into the night. Everyone in town had heard of the wonderful fabric and its amazing qualities and all were eager to see just how wise or foolish their neighbors might be.

"I should like to see how my cloth is coming along," the Emperor said to himself several days later. But when he remembered that anyone who was stupid or unfit for his office would be unable to see the marvelous fabric, he thought better of going himself. "Of course *I* will be able to see the fabric," he thought, "but I believe I shall send my honest old Minister first. He has always been fair and wise."

So the Minister was sent to call upon the weavers, and soon he arrived in the shop where the two swindlers sat working at the empty loom.

"Oh my!" he thought as he gazed upon the loom, wide-eyed. "I cannot see a single thread!" But the Minister said nothing.

"Come closer, sir!" The wily weavers graciously invited him to step up for a better look. They asked his opinion of the intricate pattern and wanted to know

if he admired the luminous colors, all the while pointing and gesturing at the empty loom.

The poor old Minister opened his eyes even wider and adjusted his spectacles, but he still couldn't see anything because, in fact, there was nothing to see. "My goodness," he thought. "Am I unfit for my royal office? How embarrassing it would be if anyone were to find out!" So he didn't dare admit that he couldn't see the miraculous fabric.

"Why . . . why, it's very pretty . . . quite, ah, enchanting!" said the old Minister, squinting. "I shall tell the Emperor that I am very pleased with it!"

"Thank you, sir." The pretend weavers beamed, and they went on to describe in great detail all the colors they had chosen and the name of their particular pattern.

The old Minister nodded and listened attentively, trying to remember every word so that he'd have something to tell the Emperor, and that is just what he did.

Soon the Emperor sent another member of his Court to see when the cloth would be ready. It was the same with this gentleman as it had been with the old Minister. He looked carefully at the loom but could see no fabric.

"Don't you think our cloth is beautiful?" gushed the swindlers. "The Minister loved it." And they pretended to run their hands across the fabric.

"I know that I am not stupid," the Officer thought. "So it must be that I am not worthy of my Imperial appointment. It's ridiculous, but for the sake of my position at Court, I must let no one know that I cannot see the cloth." So he also praised the fabric, complimenting the weavers on the rich colors and delightful design.

"Yes, Your Majesty, I, too, found the cloth enchanting!" he told the Emperor.

The whole town was talking about the wonderful cloth. At last, the Emperor went to see it for himself, accompanied by members of his Court, including the two faithful officials who had already "seen" the imaginary fabric.

"Isn't it magnificent?" cried the two royal officials. "What a splendid design! What gorgeous colors!" they said, pointing to the empty loom, for they believed that the others could truly see the cloth.

"What is this?" thought the Emperor. "I don't see a thing! Am I stupid? Am I be unfit to be Emperor? Goodness, that would be the worst thing that could ever happen to me!"

"Yes, it is indeed beautiful," said the Emperor. "It has our highest approval!" He nodded contentedly, gazing with pleasure at the empty loom. All those attending him now strained their eyes to see if they could see anything, but they saw no more than the others. Nevertheless, they all exclaimed, "It is beautiful!" just as the Emperor had, and suggested that His Majesty should have a suit of clothes made of the magnificent material in time for the upcoming procession through the town.

The swindlers sat up the entire night before the procession was to take place. They pretended to roll the fabric off the loom, pretended to cut it out with a huge pair of scissors, and stitched away with needles without thread in them. At last they declared, "Now the Emperor's new clothes are ready!"

The Emperor came in, and the scoundrels each held out an arm as if they were carrying something precious and said, "Here are Your Majesty's trousers! And your jacket! And your robe!" and so on.

"Now, would it please Your Majesty to step behind those curtains and take off your clothes," asked the scoundrels, "so that we may dress you in front of the mirror?"

So the Emperor was undressed and the swindlers pretended to fasten, lace, and button him into each new article of clothing. Meanwhile, the Emperor turned this way and that in front of the mirror.

"Oh, how wonderful Your Majesty looks in his new clothes! And how well they fit!" cried all the nobles. "What a pattern! What colors! These are indeed robes worthy of Your Majesty!"

"The canopy that is to be carried over Your Majesty in the procession is waiting outside," announced the Master of Ceremonies.

"Yes, I am quite ready," said the Emperor. "Doesn't the new suit fit well?" And he turned once more to look at himself in the mirror so that everyone might see just how much he admired the wonderful garments.

The chamberlains, who usually carried the end of the Emperor's long robe, fumbled with their hands on the ground as if they were lifting the trailing hem. They pretended to carry it as the Emperor began the procession, for they didn't dare let the people know that they could see nothing.

And so the Emperor marched, and everyone in the street who saw him and all those leaning out of windows exclaimed, "Look at how marvelous the Emperor's new clothes are! And how well they fit him!" No one said they could see nothing, for that would mean that they were unfit for office, or were simpletons.

Suddenly, from the crowd, a small child said, "But the Emperor has no clothes!"

"Good heavens," someone else said in hushed tones. "Did you hear what that child said? The Emperor has no clothes!" It started as a whisper from one person to the next, but soon everyone was talking until finally the whole crowd exclaimed, "The Emperor has no clothes!"

The Emperor himself began to worry because he was afraid they might be right. "But," he thought, "the procession must go on." And so he walked even more stiffly than before, and the chamberlains followed behind, carrying the hem of a robe that wasn't there.

The Boy Who Cried Wolf

ONCE UPON A TIME, a group of villagers hired a boy to watch over their sheep. Day in and day out, he guarded the flock as they grazed upon the hillsides beyond the village gates.

One afternoon, the shepherd boy grew tired of this job and wondered how he could liven things up. Looking down on the town from a hillside, he had an idea.

"Wolf! Wolf!" he cried. "A wolf is attacking the sheep!"

Upon hearing this, the townspeople dropped whatever they had been doing and grabbed rakes, shovels, sticks, and axes—anything that might help to protect their sheep from the hungry wolf—and ran to the boy, ready to fight.

"Ha! Ha!" The boy laughed when he saw their worried faces. "You should see yourselves. I sure fooled you!"

Grumbling, the villagers returned to the town.

The next afternoon, the boy pulled the prank again.

"Wolf! Wolf!" he cried. "Oh, it's horrible! If only someone would help me!"

Within minutes, the villagers came running, just like they had the day before.

"Ha! Ha! Ha!" The boy laughed. "Tricked you again!"

On the way back to town, the angry villagers wondered if they had hired the wrong person to protect their flock.

Shortly after the boy was left alone with the sheep, a wolf leaped out of the forest.

"Wolf! Wolf!" cried the boy. "Help! A wolf is attacking the sheep!"

The townspeople, who had just gotten back to the village, heard the cries, but they only shook their heads. "Tomorrow we'll hire someone who isn't always trying to make fools out of us," they said as they returned to their homes.

Without help, the boy was no match for the wolf, and it soon carried off all the sheep it wanted.

The boy ran to town crying, "Why didn't anyone come when I called?!"

"You should know by now, boy," said the Mayor. "No one believes a liar, even when he's telling the truth!"

The Little Red Hen

ONE DAY, the Little Red Hen and her chicks were scratching around in the barn-yard when they found a few grains of wheat. "Aha!" the hen said to her brood. "This is good fortune! If we plant this grain, by the end of the summer, we could have a nice little harvest." But she knew that if they wanted to harvest the wheat later, there was work to do now. So she gathered the grains and asked her friends if they would lend a hand.

"Who will help me plant the wheat?" asked the Little Red Hen.

"I won't!"
said the cat.

"I won't!"
said the dog.

"I won't!"
said the duck.

"Well, then I will do it myself!" said the Little Red Hen. So she found a small patch of open ground and set to work. She hoed and raked and worked the soil until it was ready, and then she planted the grain and watered it.

It wasn't long before tiny green shoots were sprouting up through the newly tilled soil. The seeds had begun to grow.

All that summer, as the sun shone and the rain fell, those tiny sprouts grew bigger and bigger. At last, they were full-grown plants with golden heads of wheat.

"Even more good fortune!" said the Little Red Hen. "The time has come to harvest our little patch!"

"Who will help me harvest the wheat?" she asked.

"I won't!" said the dog.

"I won't!" said the cat.

"I won't!" said the duck.

"Well, then I will do it myself!" said the Little Red Hen. So she took a sickle
and cut the stalks of wheat. When she was done, she gathered them into bundles
and left them to dry in the field.

Soon the wheat had dried and was ready to be threshed, to separate the edible grains from the straw.

"Who will help me thresh the wheat?" asked the Little Red Hen.

"I won't!"
said the dog.

"I won't!"
said the cat.

"I won't!"
said the duck.

"Well, then I will do it myself!" said the Little Red Hen. So she threshed the wheat and then put the grain into a burlap bag.

Now it was time to have the grain ground into flour.

"Who will help me take the grain to the mill?" asked the Little Red Hen.

"I won't!"

said the dog.

"I won't!"

said the cat.

"I won't!"

said the duck.

"Well, then I will do it myself!" said the Little Red Hen. So she loaded the bag of wheat into a wheelbarrow and took it to the mill. There, the miller ground it into fine white flour.

"How fortunate we are to have this bag of wonderful flour," said the Little Red
Hen to her chicks. "And I know just what to do with it. We should make bread!"
"Who will help me bake the bread?" asked the Little Red Hen.

"I won't!"
said the cat.

"I won't!"
said the dog.

"I won't!"
said the duck.

"Well, then I will do it myself," said the Little Red Hen, and to the flour she added milk and eggs, water and salt, a bit of sugar, some fresh butter, and yeast. Then she mixed them all together and kneaded the dough carefully. Soon it was ready to be put into a hot oven, where it was baked until it had a golden brown crust.

When the finished bread was set out to cool, it filled the air with the most glorious aroma.

"Now, who will help me eat the bread?" asked the Little Red Hen.

"I will!"
said the dog.

"I will!"
said the cat.

"I will!"
said the duck.

"Well, I wouldn't count on it!" said the Little Red Hen. "If you don't share the work, you can't share the bread!"

Then the Little Red Hen and her chicks sat down to enjoy the delicious freshly baked bread. And as they ate, they remembered the day not long ago when they had the good fortune of finding a few grains of wheat.

The Mice in Council

THE MICE HAD HAD ENOUGH. No matter where they went, whether searching for food or playing in the meadow, the cat was always a threat. It seemed he could be anywhere, silently hunting them, waiting to pounce. Something had to be done, and so a meeting was arranged.

Late one night, in a quiet corner of the barn, the anxious group was called to order. A number of suggestions were made as to how the mice should protect themselves from their enemy, the cat, but one by one, these ideas were rejected.

Finally, a mouse who was well known to everyone and well respected stepped forward. "While foraging in the trash heap the other day, I found a wonderful treasure, and I realized that all of our troubles were over. For it is this simple thing that can protect us all from that sneaky cat." He held up a small brass bell. "All we need to do is tie this bell around the cat's neck, and its tinkling sound will alert us in plenty of time for us to run away!"

The other mice cheered. Everyone agreed that the problem was now solved—everyone except a wise old mouse who had sat quietly listening. He cleared his throat and raised his paw to speak. "Friends, this does indeed sound like a wonderful plan, but I am afraid we may have overlooked one important question: Which one of us will bell the cat?"

The old mouse sat back down in silence. No one knew what to say because they realized he was right. It is one thing to talk about a plan; it is quite another to carry it out.

The Boy Who Went to the North Wind

ONCE THERE WAS A POOR WOMAN who lived on a farm with her son. One day, as she was about to make dinner, she discovered that the meal bin in the kitchen was empty. Giving her son a bowl, she asked him to go to the storage shed and fetch some more.

As he was returning to the cottage with a bowlful of meal, the cold North Wind whistled past him and sent every grain of it swirling into the air.

Frustrated, the boy went back to the shed for more meal, but upon his return the same thing happened—again, the North Wind scattered it across the countryside. For a third time, the boy repeated the process, and for a third time he watched helplessly as the careless North Wind blew away every little bit of meal that he and his mother had left.

"That's it!" he said angrily. "Mother, that greedy North Wind has taken our meal, and I intend to get it back!"

So off he went, to the land where the North Wind lives, with only enough pennies in his pocket for one night's lodging. On and on he walked, for it was a long journey from the farm to that cold and windy place. It was late the next day when the boy at last stood before the North Wind.

"Well?" demanded the icy North Wind. "What brings you to my domain?"

Gusting winds nearly knocked the boy off his feet, but he stood firm. "My mother and I are very poor, sir," the boy shouted above the roaring of the North Wind, "and yesterday, you took from my bowl the last of our meal. I need you to give it back, please, or we will starve."

"Meal?" the North Wind said. "Impossible. That meal was scattered to the four corners of the earth. But, if you are in such a bad way, maybe this will help."

Suddenly, a tablecloth tumbled out of nowhere and was blown, flapping, against the boy. He grabbed it immediately to keep it from blowing away.

"Take that tablecloth," the North Wind said as gently as he could. "Spread it over any empty table, and when you say the words 'Cloth, Cloth, bring me a feast!' it will fill the table with all the food you can eat."

The boy thanked the North Wind, folded the cloth, put it into the pocket of his ragged cloak, and started on his way back home.

Soon it was dark, and because the boy had traveled so far and still had such a long way to go, he stopped for the night at an inn.

Before going up to his room, the boy, who had not eaten for almost two days, found an empty table by the fire in the dining room.

"And would the young man like a bit of hot gruel before we close the kitchen this evening?" the Innkeeper asked as the boy sat down.

"Actually, I'd like to try out this gift I was given," the boy said. "If you don't mind."

The Innkeeper shrugged as he watched the boy take the cloth from his pocket and unfold it on the table. "Cloth, Cloth, bring me a feast!"

To the amazement of the Innkeeper and the boy, the table was instantly filled with a wonderful assortment of the most delicious-looking foods that either of them had ever seen. The boy immediately began to help himself to a leg of roasted chicken, a freshly baked roll, and a slice of hot apple pie.

"I'll just get you a napkin," the Innkeeper said as he ran to the kitchen to tell his wife what he had just seen. She happened to have been watching from the kitchen door and had also seen the miracle with her own eyes.

"Just think of the profits we could make with a cloth like that!" said the greedy Innkeeper.

"And the work it would save me!" his wife added, grinning back. Quietly, they slipped into the kitchen and closed the door behind them.

Later that night, when the inn was dark and quiet and the boy lay fast asleep in his room, a figure crept up to his bedside. There, the boy's tattered cloak hung at the foot of the bed. The figure silently pulled the magic tablecloth from the cloak's pocket and replaced it with another cloth that looked exactly like it. Then the thief crept back out of the room.

The next morning, the boy struck out early, eager to show his mother the wonderful tablecloth. On and on he walked, traveling all day so that he might make it home by dinnertime. Sure enough, he arrived just as she was about to break her last crust of bread.

"Mother," the boy cried excitedly. "You won't believe what I have brought! The North Wind gave us this wonderful tablecloth that instantly serves the most glorious food."

"I'll believe that when I see it," she said with a sigh.

The boy pulled the cloth from his pocket and, with a flourish and a snap, spread it onto the table. "Cloth, Cloth," he cried, "bring me a feast!"

But no food appeared—not even a crumb.

"Just as I thought," his mother said. "Now, do you want half of this crust of bread?"

"Why, that North Wind tricked me!" the boy cried. "Tomorrow I'll go back there and tell him to forget the magic cloth and just give me back our meal!"

And that's just what he did. By the end of the next day, he stood once again before the bitter North Wind.

"You again?" howled the North Wind. "What now?"

"The cloth, sir," the boy cried back. "It doesn't work. So if I could just get our meal back, I'll be on my way."

"Your meal is halfway around the world, boy," the North Wind roared. "But here—this should replace your loss." From behind a fir tree, a goat wafted through the air and landed before the boy. Quickly, he grabbed one of its horns to keep it from being taken by another gust of wind.

"Say to this goat, 'Goat, Goat, make me some gold!'" the North Wind said, "and it will make you enough gold that you can buy all the meal you'll ever need. Maybe then," he added under his breath, "you'll stop bothering me."

The boy thanked the North Wind, tied his belt around the goat's neck as a lead, and started on his way back home. By evening he found himself once more at the inn where he had stayed on his last journey.

"We've got a room," the Innkeeper said, "but the goat will cost you extra."

The boy, having no more money of his own, realized he could try out his latest gift.

"Goat, Goat, make me some gold!" he said, and instantly, beautiful golden coins spilled from the goat's mouth and clinked upon the inn floor. The boy scooped them up and offered two to the amazed Innkeeper. "Will this do?" he asked. Speechless, the Innkeeper could only nod as he led the boy and his goat to their room. Secretly, the Innkeeper gave his wife a sly wink, which she returned with a knowing grin.

Soon the boy was in bed and fast asleep, and once again, a figure crept into his dark room, this time leading a goat. This goat looked so much like the boy's that they could have been twins.

Quickly and quietly, the figure switched the goats,
taking the boy's and leaving the other in its place.
The boy was awake with the sun and wasted no
time making the long trip home.

"Mother," cried the boy as he reached their cottage.
"Look what the North Wind has given us! A
magic goat!"

"Hmmm," his mother said doubtfully.
"It looks like a regular goat to me."

"Just watch this!" the boy
said. "Goat, Goat, make me
some gold!"

But nothing happened. The goat only shook its head and started to eat the tablecloth.

"Oh well," the mother said. "What's another hungry mouth to feed?"

"Tricked again!" the boy cried. "This goat is supposed to make golden coins. That's it. The North Wind has to make this right!"

The next day found the boy making the all-too-familiar journey north, which was just as long and as hard as the other two had been.

"You? AGAIN?!" the North Wind roared, nearly blowing the boy over.

"Sorry, sir," the boy shouted as he struggled to hold on to his flapping cloak. "But the goat stopped making gold. Now . . . ah . . . about that meal?"

"THAT MEAL IS GONE!" bellowed the North Wind. "And I have given you my very best gifts. All I have left is this stick!"

Suddenly, a large stick came spinning out of the sky and smacked the boy on the shoulder. Quickly, he grabbed hold of it before it could follow his long-lost meal into the wind.

"Say to this stick, 'Stick, Stick, do your work!'" said the North Wind, "and it will do what it does best. Then when you wish it to stop, say, 'Stick, Stick, stop!' and it will. NOW," the North Wind roared, "GOOD-BYE!"

Grasping the final gift, the boy thanked the North Wind and scurried back the way he had come. By nightfall, he was once again at the inn.

"What? No luggage or livestock this evening?" the Innkeeper asked.

The boy handed him one of the few coins that were left from when he and the magic goat had stayed at the inn. "Just me and my stick," the boy replied.

"Follow me," the Innkeeper said, looking at his wife with raised eyebrows as they passed. She merely shrugged.

Later that night, when the inn was dark and quiet, the thieving figure once more stole into the boy's room, this time carrying a big stick, exactly like the boy's. The figure didn't know what magic a walking stick might hold, but if this boy had it, the thief thought it must be worth stealing.

By this time, the boy had grown suspicious of the Innkeeper. So instead of going to sleep, he shut his eyes and pretended to snore loudly. As the figure reached for the stick leaning in the corner near the bed, the boy suddenly stopped and cried, "Stick, Stick, do your work!"

Immediately, the stick swung into action, swatting the mysterious figure, which ran about the room crying, "Ouch! Ouch! STOP!"

The boy sat up in bed and saw the Innkeeper being chased around and around by the magic stick.

"OW! OW!" he whined. "Make it stop, and I'll give you back your tablecloth and goat!"

At sunrise the next morning, the boy was on the road heading home. He had the magic tablecloth under his arm, the lead for the magic goat in one hand, and the magic stick in the other.

His mother was amazed and delighted by the gifts he had brought. And for the rest of his days, when the boy felt the North Wind whistle past him, he touched the brim of his hat as a way of saying thank you for a table that was always full and a meal bin that was never empty.

A Note from the Artist

All of the stories and fables in this book were originally told or written by others. I simply read many versions of each and then retold them in my own words. Listed below are the original authors or the countries in which the stories are believed to have originated.

"The Ugly Duckling" and "The Emperor's New Clothes" were written by Hans Christian Andersen.

"Beauty and the Beast" was written by Gabrielle-Suzanne Barbot de Villeneuve.

"The Crow and the Pitcher," "The Boy Who Cried Wolf," and "The Mice in Council" are all attributed to Aesop.

"The Little Red Hen" is a folktale believed to have come from Russia.

"The Boy Who Went to the North Wind" is an old Scandinavian tale.

I would like to acknowledge and thank some of the people who helped to make this book possible.

First, my editor, Bridget Monroe Itkin, for her straightforward suggestions and insightful contributions, as well as her ability to work with this illustrator's ungainly schedule. And the rest of the Artisan team, including Sibylle Kazeroid, Hanh Le, Nancy Murray, Lia Ronnen, and Allison McGeehon.

My models, Hilary Barta, Karl Gustafson, Patricia Gustafson, Rachael Jenison, Cameron Klein, Rachael Mannix, and Theo Streit-Hurh, all of whom helped to bring the characters in these stories to life.

Also, Karl Gustafson for his digital expertise in adapting some of the finished images.

And last but not least, my wife, Patty: special appreciation goes to her for her design sense, technical know-how, and good counsel, not to mention her unfailing love and support. This book was truly a team effort. Thank you.